# The Ninjabread Man

# The Ninja Man

# bread

BY C. J. LEIGH

PICTURES BY
CHRIS GALL

SCHOLASTIC INC.

# Once upon a time,

there was a little old sensei who taught ninjas in a hidden dojo.

The group trained hard
to be the strongest, fastest,
smartest, and sneakiest
ninjas in all the land.

Sensei was very proud
of his students . . .

So proud that one night he made them a special treat: ninjabread.

Ninjabread was an age-old recipe passed down from sensei to sensei. It took a lifetime to master. Once baked, the cookies contained many mysterious powers.

They were also dangerously delicious.

Sensei mixed the batter, rolled the dough, and shaped the ninjabread into a tiny sword and throwing stars.

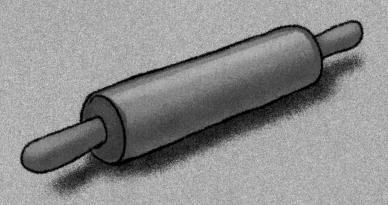

Then, Sensei crafted a Ninjabread Man.
Once done, he carefully placed the tray in the oven.

Finally, as Sensei opened the oven door to check
on the ninjabread . . .

**KA-POW!**

Out leaped the Ninjabread Man, alive and kicking!

Sensei was surprised to hear the cookie speak.

"The time has come to test your students.
Now they must try, try, as best they can.
They can't beat me, I'm the Ninjabread Man!"

With a *crack* and a *flash*, the Ninjabread Man disappeared
in a cloud of sugar dust!

Sensei sounded the gong as a warning to his ninjas.
Tonight they faced the greatest challenge of their lives.

Ninja Bear was balancing on one finger when he heard the gong.
Suddenly, a sweet scent filled the night air. Danger was near.

With a *crack* and a *flash*, a cookie figure stood
before him and announced,

"Try, try, as best as you can, you can't beat me,
I'm the Ninjabread Man!
I got past Sensei, escaped in the night,
and I'll defeat you, too, I can, I can!"

"Ninjabread Man!" shouted Ninja Bear.
"You will make a mighty morsel!"

With a running roar, Ninja Bear charged. But the Ninjabread Man jumped out of the way, and Ninja Bear lost his balance.

Then, with a bow,

the Ninjabread Man

escaped

into the

night.

"Come back!" yelled Ninja Bear. But the cookie had disappeared.

Ninja Snake was throwing stars in the forest when she sensed Sensei's warning.
The bamboo swayed in the wind. Danger was near.

Suddenly, a cookie figure stood before her and announced,

"Try, try, as best as you can, you can't beat me,
I'm the Ninjabread Man!
I got past Sensei, escaped in the night,
I dodged Ninja Bear in the pale moonlight,
and I'll defeat you, too, I can, I can!"

"Ninjabread Man!" hissed Ninja Snake. "You will make a super snack!"

With a *flick, flick, swish*, Ninja Snake launched her throwing stars. But the Ninjabread Man was too fast! He launched a cookie star ninja attack of his own.

Then, with a bow,

the Ninjabread Man

escaped

into the

night.

"Come back!" yelled Ninja Snake, but the cookie had disappeared.

Ninja Mouse was training with his sword when the warning gong rang.
Ninja Mouse heard someone tiptoeing around.
Danger was near.

In the blink of an eye, a cookie figure stood before him and announced,

"Try, try, as best as you can, you can't beat me,
I'm the Ninjabread Man!
I got past Sensei, escaped in the night,
I dodged Ninja Bear in the pale moonlight!
I slipped past Ninja Snake in a throwing-star fight!
And I'll defeat you, too, I can, I can!"

"Ninjabread Man!" squeaked Ninja Mouse. "You will make a nice nibble!"

Ninja Mouse sprang forward, but the Ninjabread Man tricked the mighty mouse.

Then, with a bow,

the Ninjabread Man

escaped

into the

night.

"Come back!" yelled Ninja Mouse, but the cookie had disappeared.

Ninja Fox was sitting beside the great waterfall. He did not hear Sensei's warning.

"Hmm," Ninja Fox gently hummed. "I sense something . . . dangerously delicious."

With a *crack* and a *flash*,
a cookie figure stood
before him and announced,

"Try, try, as best as you can, you can't beat me,
I'm the Ninjabread Man!
I got past Sensei, escaped in the night,
I dodged Ninja Bear in the pale moonlight!
I slipped past Ninja Snake and made Ninja Mouse ache!
And I'll outfox you, too, I can, I can!"

"I'm sorry," said Ninja Fox. "I didn't hear you. What did you say?"
The Ninjabread Man stepped closer and repeated,

"Try, try, as best as you can, you can't beat me,
I'm the Ninjabread Man!
I got past Sensei, escaped in the night,
I dodged Ninja Bear in the pale moonlight!
I slipped past Ninja Snake and made Ninja Mouse ache!
And I'll outfox you, I can, I can!"

"I'm so sorry," said Ninja Fox, pretending he could not hear
the cookie. "The waterfall is so loud. What did you say?"

The Ninjabread Man
took one final step closer.

Following one quick movement, a cloud of sugar dust covered Ninja Fox.

Ninja Bear, Ninja Snake, and Ninja Mouse
came running out of the forest to find Ninja Fox.
Was the Ninjabread Man gone?

Far away, in another hidden dojo, a little old
sensei worked under the mystical moon—mixing,
rolling, and shaping . . .
a Ninjabread Man.

# Ninjabread cookies

**SIFT INTO A BOWL AND MIX:**
2-1/2 cups all-purpose flour
I teaspoon baking powder
1/4 teaspoon baking soda
1/4 teaspoon salt

I teaspoon ground cinnamon
I teaspoon ground ginger
I teaspoon ground cloves
1/4 teaspoon ground allspice

**BEAT TOGETHER IN ANOTHER BOWL:**
I farm-fresh egg
2/3 cup dark molasses
I cup firmly packed dark brown sugar
6 tablespoons softened butter

Add dry ingredients slowly to wet mixture until well blended. Cover and refrigerate for one hour. Preheat oven to 350°F. Sift flour onto your board and your rolling pin as you work to keep the dough from sticking. Roll out a portion of dough 1/4 inch thick. Cut out your gingerbread men with a two-inch floured cookie cutter. Or, with floured hands, shape and hand press your own little gingerbread men. (One way to shape them is to make a little ball for the head, a larger ball for the body, and stick-shaped rolls for the arms and legs.) Place one inch apart on a buttered cookie sheet. Bake 8 minutes, or until slightly firm to touch. Cool on wire rack. Decorate with frosting, raisins, and candies to create your own Ninjabread cookies. This will make about 50 cookies. **MAKE SURE YOU HAVE A GROWN-UP HELP YOU!**

# Glossary

**bamboo:** A kind of tall plant
**chomp:** To bite or chew on something
**dojo:** A school for martial arts
**gong:** A big metal disc that makes a loud sound when it is hit
**morsel:** A small piece of food
**sensei:** Someone who teaches martial arts

To Ninja Crow, who knows who he is and who is what he knows —CJL

For Cormac—who recently popped out of the oven —CG

Text copyright © 2016 by Scholastic Inc. • Illustrations copyright © 2016 by Chris Gall • All rights reserved. Published by Scholastic Inc., *Publishers since 1920.* SCHOLASTIC and associated logos are trademarks and/or registered trademarks of Scholastic Inc. • The publisher does not have any control over and does not assume any responsibility for author or third-party websites or their content. • No part of this publication may be reproduced, stored in a retrieval system, or transmitted in any form or by any means, electronic, mechanical, photocopying, recording, or otherwise, without written permission of the publisher. For information regarding permission, write to Scholastic Inc., Attention: Permissions Department, 557 Broadway, New York, NY 10012. • This book is a work of fiction. Names, characters, places, and incidents are either the product of the author's imagination or are used fictitiously, and any resemblance to actual persons, living or dead, business establishments, events, or locales is entirely coincidental.• ISBN 978-1-338-12996-0 • 10 9 8 7 6 5 4 3 2    16 17 18 19 20 • Printed in the U.S.A. 40 • First printing 2016 • The text type was set in Gill Sans Bold. • The display type was set in Amelia BT Regular. Art direction and book design by Marijka Kostiw